GIGANTOSAURUS™

Try Again, TINY

templar
books

A TEMPLAR BOOK

This book is based on the episode *Because Triceratops* from the TV series *Gigantosaurus* ™.
Screenplay by Annabelle Perichon.
The TV series *Gigantosaurus* ™ is created and produced by Cyber Group Studios.
Based on the original characters created by Jonny Duddle in the book *Gigantosaurus*,
first published by Templar Books in 2014.

First published in the UK by Templar Books, an imprint of Bonnier Books UK
The Plaza, 535 King's Road, London SW10 0SZ
Owned by Bonnier Books, Sveavägen 56, Stockholm, Sweden

ISBN 978-1-78741-598-0

Adapted by Harriet Paul
Edited by Lydia Watson & Carly Blake
Designed by Dynamo Ltd.
Additional design by Adam Allori
Production Controller: Ché Creasey

Printed in China

Tiny has hidden **10** of her
favourite flowers
throughout the book.

Can you find them all?

This story is all about **TINY**, the little triceratops who's LOTS of fun. Tiny loves nothing more than dancing, singing and telling jokes, so she struggles to take her very important DINO TEST seriously! Will Tiny have to change her fun-loving ways to fit in with the rest of the triceratops herd?

The four friends were busy with one of their favourite activities – Giganto-watching! Rocky stood on Mazu, who stood on Bill, and holding them all up was Tiny. Even though she was the smallest, Tiny was one STRONG dinosaur!

Suddenly, the tower wobbled dangerously. Was it an earthquake? Or worse, a GROUNDWOBBLER?

No, it was just Tiny, performing some of *her* favourite activities ... singing and dancing!

Hey, careful down there!

It's not me, it's Tiny!

Bill must be moving!

Oh, life *is* FUN and FUN *is* TOPS, when *you're* a TRI-CERA-TOPS!

"This is not the time to mess around, Tiny! Giganto will hear us!" Mazu hissed.

Sure enough, the mighty dinosaur took a giant STOMP towards them, and their shaky tower tumbled to the ground.

THUD! The dinos landed in a heap right in front of Tiny's big brother, Trey.

Trey chuckled as he helped Rocky, Bill, Tiny and Mazu to their feet. "I'm glad I bumped into you, sis. I've been looking all over Cretacia for you!"

Tiny explained that they had been hiding from Giganto. Trey looked at her in disbelief.

You're a TRICERATOPS!

"YOU don't need to hide from anyone," he told her.
"We triceratops are a brave and strong herd of WARRIORS!"

Tiny wasn't so sure. "I'm actually a better dancer than a warrior," she said. She did a little dance to show her brother what she could do, but Trey just laughed.

Look at my awesome moves!

"No time for that," he said. "We need to prepare for your TRICERATOPS TRIAL!" Trey was going to teach Tiny all the skills she needed to be part of the herd.

"Every triceratops has to complete this special test to prove their strength," said Trey. "First, the DEAD TREE TACKLE."

Trey used his powerful horns to uproot a big old tree. It fell to the ground with a CRASH!

"How about YOU tackle the tree and then I DECORATE it?" suggested Tiny.

Let's make it look pretty!

Tiny loved to draw and decorate
almost as much as she loved dancing!

"Very funny, sis," replied Trey.
But Tiny wasn't joking – for once!

"Next, we do the STOMPS," said Trey. He jumped UP into the air . . . and landed with a mighty THUMP that sent the smaller dinos flying! They all giggled as they bounced up and down.

Then it was Tiny's turn. She tried to stomp just like Trey had showed her.

It wasn't long before Tiny had turned the moves into
a brilliant breakdance! Her friends cheered as she hopped,
bopped and swung her tail, before finishing with a head spin.
Trey was not impressed.

After the STOMPS, it was time for the TRICERATOPS TUG. "Grab my horn and see if you can get me to budge," Trey instructed Tiny.

But Trey was too BIG and HEAVY! Instead, Tiny jumped on Trey's back and began to sing, but Trey quickly put a stop to that.

Poor Tiny DID want to take the trial seriously, but she couldn't help turning it into something fun.

Tree tackle and toss, then tug and stomp, the Triceratops Trial – what a romp!

Triceratops do not do FUN!

"Triceratops are STRONG. We like to push BIG things around. And we are VERY SERIOUS about it!" Trey said.

"If you don't pass the trial, you'll have to spend more time with the herd learning the triceratops ways," Trey warned his sister. "That means less time with your friends!"

Now Tiny was nervous. Her friends were more important to her than ANYTHING.

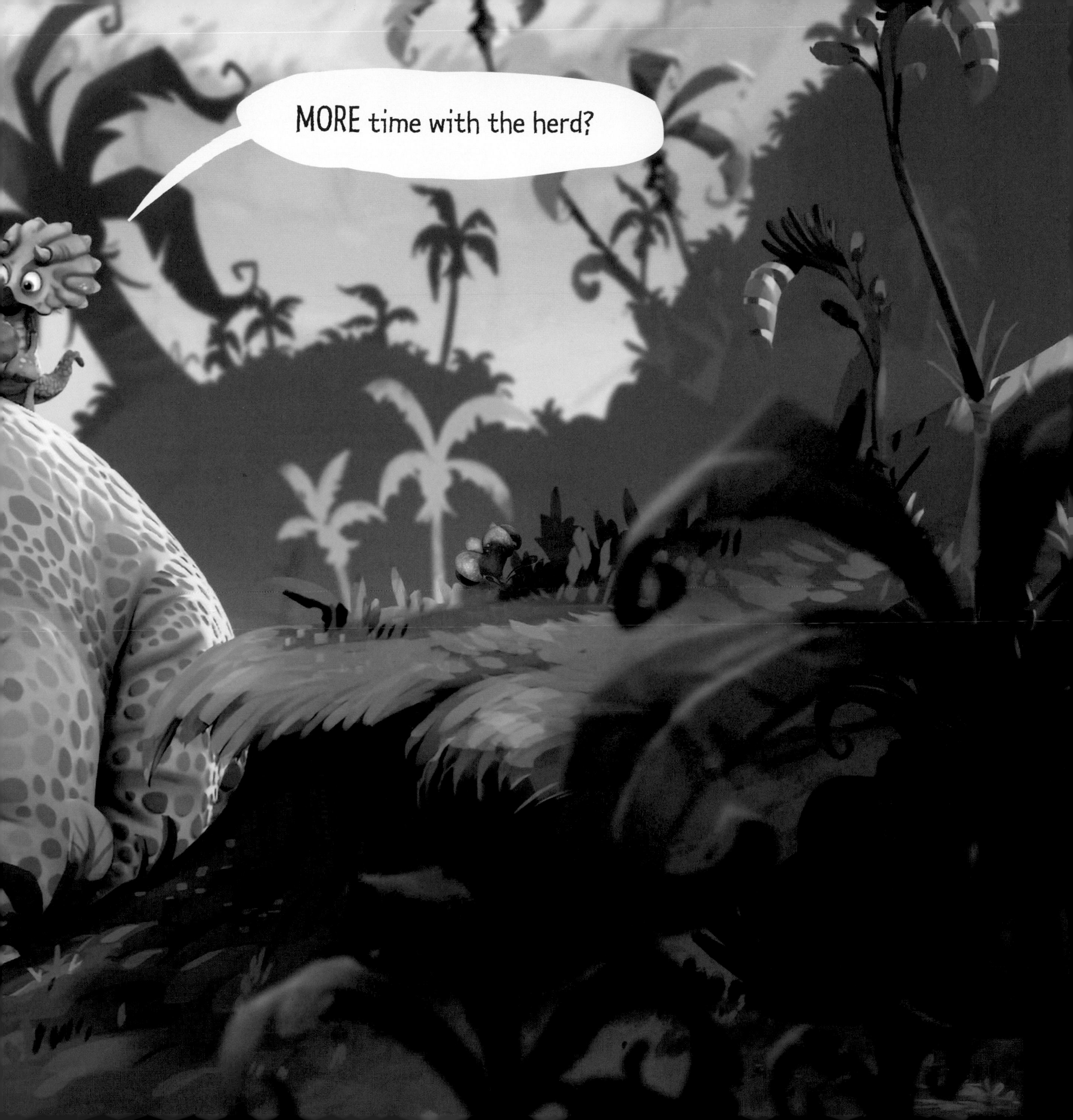
MORE time with the herd?

Trey showed Tiny the final triceratops skill, the TREE TOSS.
But instead of throwing the tree, Tiny wedged one end under Trey's
foot and used it as a see-saw to fling HERSELF into the air!

"Look who's flying now!" Tiny shouted as she sailed through the sky,
before landing with a flourish in front of her brother.

"That's enough!" Trey said sternly. "If you don't get serious, you'll never pass the Triceratops Trial!"

"Sorry, Trey," said Tiny. "I do WANT to be a good triceratops, but I can't help doing things my own way."

There's only one way to do things – the RIGHT way!

All of a sudden, there was a loud ROAR behind them . . .

GIGANTOSAURUS!

All the commotion had disturbed Giganto, and he did NOT look happy! He quickly spotted the little dinos and came thundering towards them.

RUUUUN!

Tiny, Rocky, Mazu and Bill raced through the jungle until Giganto's STOMPS were well behind them. THEY were safe, but they'd lost Trey!

They retraced their steps and found him stuck in quicksand – and he was sinking! The four friends needed to figure out how to save him, and fast.

It looks like this swamp really likes me!

Don't worry! We'll get you out!

Tiny tried to TUG Trey
out, but it was no good.
Then she had a better idea.
She TACKLED a nearby tree
to the ground and TOSSED
it next to her brother.

"Looks like you learned
a thing or two after all,"
said Trey.

Nicely done, little sis!

The four little dinosaurs slid the tree trunk underneath Trey and jumped onto one end. Trey was catapulted out of the quicksand. It worked just like the tree see-saw that Tiny had made earlier!

At last, Trey was safely on solid ground. "You did it!" he said to Tiny proudly. "And you did it YOUR way."

Can you get off us now?

Later that day, Trey gathered the herd together. It was time to watch Tiny's Triceratops Trial! They waited silently for it to begin.

"Welcome, fellow triceratops warriors! My sister, Tiny, is one of the bravest in all Cretacia," Trey said proudly. "She's strong enough to pull me out of quicksand, and she performs our trial tasks like no one else!"

Trey turned to his sister, who was looking anxious.
He wished her luck – but he knew she didn't really need it.

Tiny took a deep breath and stepped out in front of the herd.
It was show time! Would all her practice pay off?

First up, Tiny fiercely TACKLED and TOSSED a tree.

Then she showed her strength in STOMPING and TUGGING.

Of course, she completed each task with her own special Tiny touch!

When she had finished, there was a LONG pause . . . before the triceratops herd began to stomp their feet in approval.

Tiny had passed! There was only one way to celebrate – with a dance of course. And this time, even Trey joined in!

That was how Tiny learned that she didn't need to change to get the approval of her herd. With her own special Tiny touch, she proved that being different can be a good thing, after all! Tiny even found that she CAN be serious sometimes . . . serious about having fun, that is!

What does a triceratops sit on?
Its TRICERA-BOTTOM!

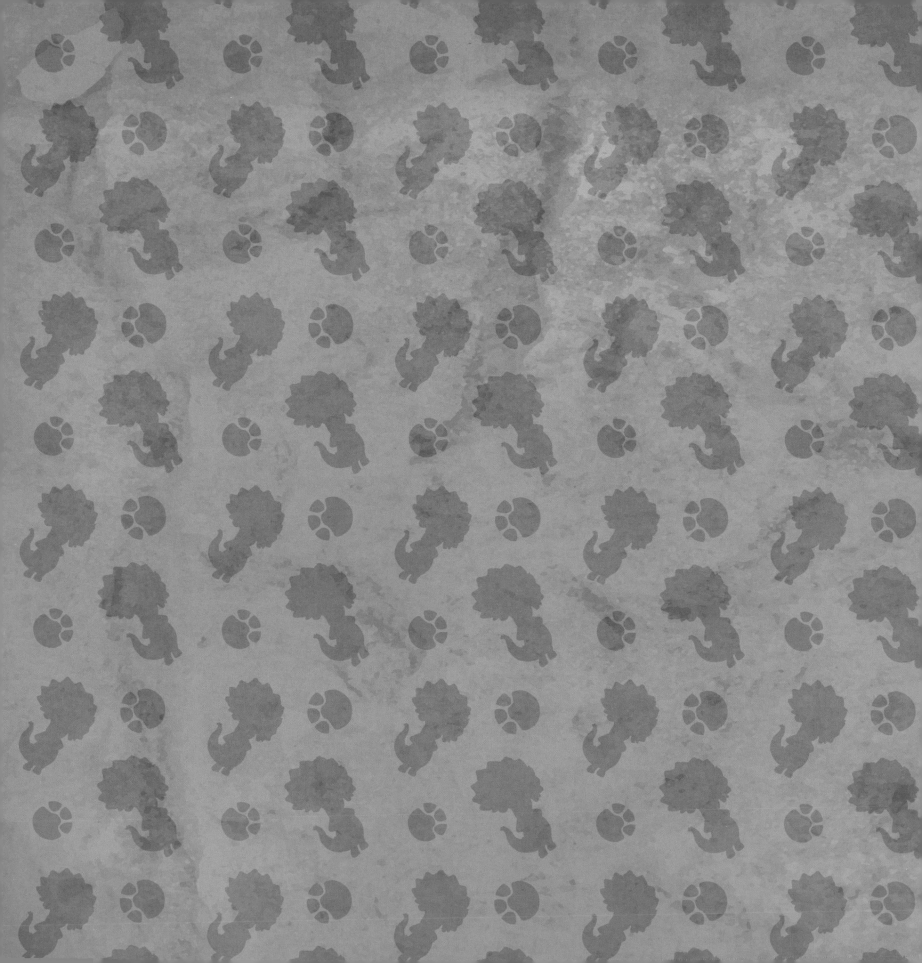